SUNSHINE

L. T. Emery

First Edition
Published
Nordic Press
Chronicles Imprint
Kindlyckevägen 13
Rimforsa, Sweden. 2022

This is a work of fiction. Similarities to real people,
places, or events
Are entirely coincidental

Sunshine by
L.T. Emery
978-91-987509-4-2
Cover Design and illustration by
Womba Dream
Formatted by
C. Marry Hultman
Edited by
Derek Power

For Robyn,
My little ray of sunshine

Chapter 1

This all started a long, long time ago, but for me, I guess it started with the boy in the dump. That was ten years ago now when the cars still flew, and we were still reaching for the stars. The world had already started to fall, not that we knew it.

"If my pa catches you here, again, you'll be in for it," the boy said and coughed. It was a horrible chesty cough that came from deep down in his lungs. "Whatcha lookin' for?"

I looked around to see it was the Dump Master's son, "Looking for sunshine."

"I'd love to see the sunshine. I'm seven

and ain't never seen a glint of sunshine!"

No one had since the Smog rolled in about two hundred years ago. The stories say that society woke one morning up to a world cloaked in fog. A fog that never cleared. No one knows where it comes from or why it happened. Some say it was wrath thrown down by God. The Russians thought it was the yanks. The yanks thought it was the Russians. Others thought it was a science experiment gone wrong. Most thought it was the Earth fighting back against all the pollution we kicked into the atmosphere. Doesn't really matter what caused it, though, does it? The end result is the same.

"You ain't gonna find any sunshine he-" The boy was cut off by another chesty cough. With this, I knew the poor kid had The Bronch.

After the Smog rolled in, people just accepted it, adapted to life alongside it; after all, it would clear soon enough, they all thought. It wasn't long until the world realised it had more pressing things to worry about then not being able to see more than twenty yards in front of you. That maybe a little bit of an overreaction, the Smog's thickness varied; at its worst, it would be twenty yards or even less, but most of the time there was a good couple of hundred yards-worth of visibility. People started dying and fast. The Smog, as people came to call it, had some horrible shit in it that causes *The Bronch*. People's lungs to become infected, they fill up with mucus, and if you're lucky you'll drown to death. If not, then The Bronch goes to your brain, you become confused, start to lose yourself, before falling into a coma and... that's all she wrote.

I was lucky; I had a filter mask, an A-shaped suction cup that went over your nose and mouth, they had this filter connected to them by a small cable that sat behind your ear. They were clear, so people could still see your face and your expressions. They cleared the Smog from the air you breathed, made it safe. Everyone wore these, if you could afford them. They were designed and mass-produced soon after the Smog descended. I couldn't afford one, but at fourteen, I was something of a prodigy, my brain was just wired knowing how to make things work, knowing how to fix things. I found, fixed, and sold these to make a small amount of money.

The kid would be dead before the year

was out, and even now, I wonder why I didn't give him one. I guess it's because he already had The Bronch, and no filter would have fixed him.

"I know I'm not gonna find sunshine here," I said, looking up into the gloomy, grey, "but if I find a working flux gear in all this junk, then my rocket will take me up above the smog and into the sunshine," I finished, kicking away a broken hoverboard.

"You don't have no rocket. You just a kid like me."

The boy was annoying, but I tolerated him. Even knowing he didn't have long left; the kid was friendly and kind. He'd helped me get away from the Dump Master's robot guard dogs several times.

"I'm twice your age, kid. I have a rocket built and ready to go. I just need the flux gear and... BLAST-OFF!" I shouted, making the kid jump.

"Hey!" he whined, looking close to tears.

I felt a twinge of conscience. "I'm sorry," I said. "I'm Cyra, come on, help me look, and maybe I'll take you up with me. There's a spare seat, you know." There wasn't, but I needed all the help I could get.

"Really?"

"We'll see," I said.

We both went about poking through the junkyard on the hunt for a working flux gear. There were mountains of junk to pick through; piles of scrap sat atop broken down hovercars. There were rows of disused hydrogen pumps next to walls of dusty refrigerators. It was a dangerous game, and we had to be careful not to cause an avalanche of rubbish as we picked.

"Cyra! I got one," The kid shouted a while later.

I ran over to the kid, pulling out my universal tester as I went. "Oh, great find," I said and patted him on the back.

It looked to be in great nick. I set up the tester and grinned at the kid, "Here goes."

Silence. The all-important buzz of life never came. I tried again and again, but nothing. Forlorn, I threw the flux gear to the floor. "Maybe next t-"

A crash came from behind a huge pile of electrical junk; my eyes widened in knowing horror. The robot guard dogs had found me.

"Cyra, hide!"

My eyes darted around the dump, and within the limited visibility, I spotted an industrial-sized washing machine. I ran to it, climbed inside, and pulled the door to, watching the kid through the dusty, glass door.

"Ace. Bowser. Down." He shouted. The dogs were built to resemble Dobermanns, but they were completely metallic, except for their feet that had some sort of hardwearing rubber to help them grip the floor as they ran, much like the old tires that cars used to have. The two dogs sat at his command, closing their razor-sharp metal teeth lined jaws and I saw they had had their left ears clipped with v's indenting their tips; this was a sort of brand to couple them to this yard. They were programmed not to harm him, and he led them away, throwing a wave my way as he went.

The boy saved me again, I thought from within the machine. I owe him one, and I know just the thing.

It was then that a glinting light caught my attention from the corner of my eye. Light poured down on something metal. I looked up, through the dusty washing machine door to the sky, to the source of the light, only to have it disappear. Was that sunlight?

I climbed out of the washing machine, and wandered to the metal object, quickening my step as I went, hoping it was what I thought it was. Exhilaration and hope filled me all at once; it was another flux gear. Tester at the ready, I pulled it free and whispered a prayer. The buzz confirmed this one worked.

It took me two days to fit the flux gear and finish readying my rocket. It had taken me a year to put together. I lived with my parents on a small farm on the outskirts of Cell City, a sprawling metropolis that reached far into the sky. The cities built up, hoping to climb above the Smog and reach the sky. It never happened, though.

The farm brought in some money; we were in no way rich, but at least we ate well. Since the Smog rolled in, fresh food was hard to come by. The low light meant few crops could grow. We specialised in chard but even managed a few stunted carrots. The main food source for the world now was mushrooms. Mushrooms for breakfast, mushrooms for lunch, mushrooms for dinner, and dessert.

The fact we had the farm meant I had

room to have a workshop in one of the massive sheds, and it was in there I built the rocket, a squat thing, but it packed a punch and thanks to a test run I knew it would go high enough to break through the Smog and into the sunshine.

When I finished the rocket, I returned once more to the dump. I climbed the fence in my usual spot where the barbed wire was missing and into the yard. I found the boy in one of the wide paths that the dredgers use; he was playing on the broken hoverboard, pretending he was zooming through the streets and parks of Cell City. He acted like he was going around the loops and the over the jumps of the hover parks, laughing as he did, until he wasn't laughing but instead coughing his guts up, drowning on his own mucus. I don't mind telling you that that brought a tear to my eye. I composed myself before I went to him.

"Hey!" I shouted to him, "Wanna see some sunshine?" The boy's face lit up, beaming as bright as the sun; that was all the sunshine I needed.

The trip went fine. He went up, he saw the sun, and he came down again. He died two weeks later, and it was that night when things really went to shit.

Chapter 2

Even when I was readying the rocket, I heard rumours of the cities falling. Of society beginning to fall apart, although we never really knew why. We could hear explosions off in the distance but had no idea what was happening in Cell City, and all around the globe. We all knew that things had slowly been in decline, the population was waning. If you didn't have money, you didn't have a mask, and if you didn't have a mask, you'd soon be dead. Resources were on the decline too, but through a morbid sort of luck, things stayed okay. Fewer people and fewer resources evened themselves out. Sure, people were unhappy. Society screamed for a solution to the Smog, or at least a cure or immunisation against The Bronch. There were always rumours that one or the other was coming, but nothing ever materialised.

Society tipped though, and within a year the world was a wasteland, a constant fight for survival against something none of us ever expected.

I remember when it hit us, I was lying in bed the night after the boy had died. It was only me and Vic, the boy's dad, who saw him off. Vic cremated him in the dump's incinerator. "This was the only place he called home, and here he shall stay," Vic had said. He was a big man, barrel-chested, with a big bushy beard and massive dinner plate hands. He was a scary man to be on the wrong side of, and it was the first time he spoke to me, rather than cursing and chasing me out of the dump. "You ever need anything; you just ask me," he said and thanked me for making the boy truly happy just once.

I was looking at my bedroom ceiling in the dead of night, thinking about the happiness that had twinkled in his eyes two weeks earlier when he'd gone up into the sky, and then the emptiness in them as he lay dead waiting for the incinerator. I wanted to bring that twinkle, that spark, to everyone's eyes. I was always so narrow-minded in my scope; a one-man rocket just to see the sunshine, masks to save just one person. Why not use the knowledge and skills I had to try and fix it all? Why not do what LexGo Corp, Circe Pharmaceuticals, and the rest of the oligarchy couldn't? That's when the howling started.

It was a sound so unexpected; my mind couldn't comprehend what I was hearing. The howl was in no way animalistic; it was entirely human and almost childish. It was the howl of a teen pretending to be a werewolf.

The howling was coming from my parents' room, and within a second of it starting, my mother's screams joined the cacophony. It was so loud and so piercing that it hurt my ears. Chills ran down my spine, but despite the fear, I ran to their room just down the dim hall and burst in. What I saw was imprinted in my mind for all eternity.

Two men loomed over my parents. They were all but naked except for the threadbare shorts and tattered shoes they wore. One man was holding down my dad, howling like a dog in heat, while the other slit his throat with a kitchen knife. All the while, my mum just sat paralysed, screaming over and over until it became nothing but a hoarse, harsh whisper. I remember the glint from the lamp next to the bed bouncing off the blade and into my eyes and wondering why these men would take the time to turn it on. I remember noticing how the knife was not one of ours; I thought, they specifically came here to do this.

I didn't want to watch what was unfolding in front of me, but I was powerless to turn away. I couldn't feel my legs, I couldn't feel anything; it was like an out of body experience. I watched the blood spray from my dad's throat, showering the two men, pumping out in two, three, four beats of my dad's heart. Its final beats. I watched as a frenzy took over them, and they both lapped up the blood. They acted like men just out of the desert without water for days, slurping the steaming blood straight from dad's neck. They drank as if their lives depended on it, and I guess they did. I watched as two mythical creatures fed on my dad. Then

I snapped out of my paralysis.

I ran into the bedroom and grabbed Mum's hand, tried to pull her from the bed, but her hand, slick with blood, just slipped straight through.

"Mum!" I screamed.

Light flickered back into her eyes, and I grabbed her wrist that time and dragged her from the bed. We ran from the room, the men didn't even notice us, such was their need for blood. Down the stairs we went and out the back door, into the waiting Smog.

Two more men, similarly dressed, met us on the porch, and we bumped straight into them before we had a chance to stop ourselves.

"Aha, dinner is served," one of the men said. You'd expect a vampire to hiss or snarl or growl when they speak, but no, he spoke like any normal person would, albeit devoid of any emotion. What they lacked in terrifying voices was made up in their eyes. I hadn't noticed it before, but this close, I saw their eyes lacked any real colour. Their irises were a metallic silver, so lacking in humanity it bordered on machine.

They grabbed us both. One man pinned

my arm behind my back and began to lead me off the porch and away.

"Mum," I screamed, reaching my free arm back toward her like she would save me. I was terrified; I'd just watched my dad die the most horrendous death and knew they had similar plans for me. Maybe it was my scream or the look of utter terror in my eyes, but that's when something came over Mum. Some maternal instinct took her over. You used to hear about these massive feats of strength from parents; like a parent lifting a broken-down hover-bus off their kid singlehandedly. Well, that's what my mum did then; she fought herself free from her captor, somehow throwing him off her, over the porch railing and into the drying remains of a thorny bush. She leapt from the porch landing onto the man who had hold of me and began scratching at his eyes. He dropped me and started to flail around, trying to get at her.

"Cyra, run!" she screamed.

And I did. I ran for my workshop, the place I knew best, the place with a million and one nooks and crannies, places I could stay hidden in for a long time. I looked over my shoulder just once to see mum clinging to the back of my captor, her thumb deep in his eye socket, blood and a clear goop dripping down her forearm and onto her nightdress. I watched as the other man, now free of the bush, grabbed her by the hair and viciously slammed her into the muddy ground. I watched as he stamped on her head with a sickening thud, and then I could watch no more. The tears in my eyes and the thickening Smog made it all but impossible; I ran to my workshop.

Inside, I looked around for a place to hide, there were storage cupboards, shelving, a second floor, and even a small cellar I could hide in, but something else caught my attention instead. Revenge. I may have only been 14 at the time, but I knew these things wouldn't stop with my parents. They'd come for me sooner or later.

The day after the kid went into the sky, I retrieved what I could of the rocket and started to build again. I still wanted to see the sunshine and what was another year of building? The rockets themselves had unfortunately been lost, but I'd started work on another, smaller, more powerful design. It sat on my workbench; one look at it and I knew what I was going to do.

I flicked off the locks on the wheels at the base of each leg of the worktable and wheeled it facing the entrance I just came in. I didn't have any of the high-grade fuel needed to propel me above the Smog, but I did have a can of plain old petrol to hand, and that would do for what I needed. I emptied the can into the fuel reservoir and primed the ignition. One click of a button was all it needed now.

The waiting was beyond excruciating. I could have been there, stood at the worktable, finger on the button for two minutes or two hours when the howling started again. I jumped out of my skin and very nearly switched the rocket on at that moment.

"Come on out, darling, we won't hurt you," one of the men said, he sounded almost posh. Then the doors flung open with a bang.

I flicked the switch on the rocket. There was a brief whizz as the motor powered up, then the roar was deafening. I could only stand to watch for a second before the blaze was too much, and even then, I was seeing white for at least an hour.

The flames kicked out of the rocket, engulfing the first two men who entered. They went up so quick it looked like a million tiny bombs all exploded at once; they didn't even have the time to scream. The other two behind had differing luck. The flames punched the man who was howling and calling out to me, knocking him back, catching his left side aflame. His scream was as piercing as that of my mum's, but this one I liked. The other guy, the one my mum maimed, leaving him with one eye, was lucky, and the flame narrowly missed him altogether.

I had to look away after that, but I still managed to glimpse the workbench fly through my workshop, propelled by the killer flames, smashing into and through the wood wall, and out into the night.

I heard the screaming and commotion outside the barn continue. I heard One-eye try to extinguish Howler. I heard Howler scream and scream, and I hoped his skin was cooked and dripping off him. I finally heard the screams start to peter out just before one of them; I think it was Howler, cried, "We'll get you for this!"

After the racket had ceased, I found a spare mask in the workshop and strapped it on.

Briefly, breathing in the Smog wasn't a massive risk, but I didn't want to be breathing it in all night. I also noted that the vampires didn't wear masks at all, so they either weren't afflicted with The Bronch, or they simply didn't care.

I stayed in the workshop for the rest of the night, curled up, shaking. It dawned on me then that I was an orphan. My parents were dead. I was alone. I'd lost everything I'd known and loved in this life and had no idea what I'd do with myself next. I cried my eyes out in racking sobs, until exhaustion tipped me into sleep.

Chapter 3

Light just seems to brighten in the mornings, like a dimmer switch to the world is slowly being turned up. I've seen paintings of sunrises, where piercing light streams out over the horizon, brightening everything it touches—bringing warmth and security with it. Now, that image seemed to be more of a myth than the fucking vampires that feasted on my parents. I didn't have the same level of resolve then, didn't have all of the fight in me like I do now, but it came real quick.

When the day's gloom meant I could see the house from the workshop without the need for lights and my tears had finally dried up, I left. Mum was lying dead outside the house, her throat slit just like my dad's. There was a little blood on her nightgown, mostly my dad's, and dotted on the floor around her, but she was pretty clean, all things considered. I had expected to see an utter bloodbath, but the vampires really got their fill.

Even after a night of crying, the tears came again. I dropped to my knees and rested my head on my mum's bosom, the way I would have a few years earlier before I grew up. I wished I'd not stopped at that moment. After a while, I composed myself, told her I loved her, and kissed her on the cheek.

Dad was a different scene. That was a blood bath. The blood spattered the walls and carpet and the bedsheets. Dad again was pretty clean, though. I hugged him and immediately wished I hadn't. The cold, hard, lifeless body was not the man that used to hug me so tightly it hurt. I cried some more and hugged him even harder, despite my emotional pain.

I tried to call the police, but the phones were out. I expected them to come the night before with all the noise my rocket would have made, but of course, my experience was just the same as millions of others all around the globe. Vampires, a creature from fiction, had risen up and pulled the world down. I only had one person I could turn to.

***

The walk to the dump was the loneliest of my life. I navigated the misty morning, the Smog getting thicker with every step I took. One of the things you learnt pretty quick was to get around with very little visibility, so it wasn't a problem for me getting where I was going. I saw so many bodies on that walk; people drained dry, I even saw a small herd of cattle all slaughtered, bleed out. In the end, I just stopped looking around, but the screams reaching out like tentacles from the unknown dark depths of the ocean still found my ears, and that equalled the terror I felt hearing the howl the night before. Seemingly, from every house I passed, the awful screams and commotions were heard over and over.

I look back now, knowing it was a miracle a vampire didn't stumble across me.

I reached the dump, pressed the buzzer

for entrance and waited. Gone were the days where I needed to hop the fence.

I waited a while, and there was no response, so I buzzed again. I looked around me; the hairs on the back of my back stood to attention. I had the ominous feeling that eyes were watching me through the gloom. I pressed the buzzer again, over and over, then held it down. The dirge of the buzz rising until I felt something would jump out and grab me.

Then a voice from the intercom, "Get the fuck outta here!" the gruff man said.

"Wait! Vic, it's me. It's me, Cyra."

"The hell are you doing here? You seen what's going on out there?"

"Please, let me in," I pleaded. "I have nowhere left to go." A moment passed, where nothing happened. "You promised."

The lock on the gate clicked, and it started to slowly roll open.

"You better shut that behind you," the voice through the intercom said.

I slipped inside and then rolled the gate shut behind me, waiting for the click of the lock to snap back into place.

I looked out into the grey, I expected shining silver eyes to pierce the murk and glare back at me, but nothing appeared.

No sooner had I started to make my way to the house than I heard the robot guard dogs bounding up to me.

Before I could see them, I shouted, "Ace. Bowser. Down," Just like the boy had. Vic had updated them to recognise my voice, and as soon as I spoke, they went silent. A few more steps, and I saw them both sitting like real dogs, on their haunches. "Hey guys," I said, walking between the two, patting them on their cold heads. "Go, guard the gate."

They slunk off toward the gates, where I knew they'd sit sentinel, protecting us.

I walked through the yard until the house began to appear through the thinning Smog.

Vic sat on the porch, on his rocker, shotgun in hand, "The hell happened to you?"

I sat next to him, on what was his son's rocker, and told him what happened the night before.

He said nothing throughout, but when I was finished, he ran a hand threw his beard, lowered his head, and shook it slightly. "I'm sorry, Cyra," he said. "You gotta home here."

Chapter 4

And so, as the world slowly died, everything that made life easy slowly broke down too. The internet died first. Electricity was next, then the running water. The generators died when the petrol ran out, and when the batteries died, all we had left was wind up flashlights and those little solar-powered garden lights. We were lucky, and thanks to some wind turbines I managed to keep the lights on, the water hot, and the ice solid, at least for the most part.

The next ten years went by without too much to note. Vic and I were always amiable to each other, but we never grew all that close. I appreciated him for putting a roof over my head, for feeding me, for giving me safety in these crazy times, but he always seemed angry, not with me, but because of that hole in his life. He lost his wife; she died during childbirth, then he lost his son thanks to The Bronch. We shared that hole our lost families caused. We also shared that anger.

Our lives rolled on. Priority number one was fortifying the dump. With my engineering skills, the mountains of crap, and Vic's help, we made the place pretty much impenetrable to the vampires. We also had Ace and Bowser on our side.

We alternated taking one of the mutts with us on food and medicine runs. Vampires would try their luck with us in the early days, but the jaws of Ace and Bowser ripped the vampires to shreds, and they tended to leave us be unless they were really hungry.

Over the course of ten years and tens of attempts to take us, we soon learned these vampires weren't like those in the media. They were not allergic to garlic. They didn't burst into flame when a wooden stake was thrust through their heart. They didn't scream in unbearable pain when coming into contact with Christian paraphernalia. They were very human; they could be killed just the same as you and me. They did have a heightened healing factor, they were stronger and faster than the average, and of course, they had their silver eyes. Eyes that could see through the Smog. Eyes they used to get the drop on Vic during one food run. Vic came back in a bad shape; he'd badly sprained an ankle during the chase. He only made it back thanks to Bowser; the dog fought off many vampires, allowing Vic to escape. Bowser never returned, we don't know what happened to him, but Vic thinks they overpowered the robot in numbers and pulled it to bits.

We never found out where the vampires came from or why they spouted up overnight. But I would. Later.

When I wasn't off scavenging or working on keeping us safe, I was still striving for sunshine. Sunshine for all. That's what I wanted. There was room at the dump for me to get a new workshop in place. Once it was up and running, I started to turn my eyes to science, trying to find a way to clear the Smog. I started by trying to make bigger, more effective masks, but it didn't work. I was good with tools and building things but when it came to fixing the world's problems, I fell short, and I became angry and withdrawn. I became so addicted to the fix I ended up forgetting to wear my mask. I'd be forever taking it off, inspecting it, looking for a new angle to use. The only thing I found was The Bronch.

Chapter 5

That first, knowing cough came the same day I found the boy's stash, the same day I left Vic. It was autumn, the days were chilly, and the nights were cold. I was digging around a corner of the dump I'd neglected a little more than the rest in hopes of finding some more filters I could work on. I happened upon an old refrigerator. I had seen it before, a big old red thing with the word ZMEG written across the middle, but I'd never opened the thing. Why would I? All I could hope to find in there was the sickly stench of off food, but for whatever reason this time, my mind was elsewhere, above the Smog, soaring through the clear skies, no doubt, and I absentmindedly opened the thing.

My breath was immediately taken away. I looked in to see the gloves I'd given the boy for his trip above the Smog. They were sat neatly arranged on top of a few, tattered old hardback books. I picked up the gloves feeding them from hand to hand, remembering the day he'd gone up.

The boy sat in the capsule; I was doing up the safety harnesses, checking them thrice. There were no controls in the capsule—I'd automated everything; one button would kick things off, and the computers would handle the rest—there was just one small window to look out of. As I was finishing off the safety checks, I gave him a pair of thick, black thermal gloves. They'd keep his hands warm during the trip.

"Cyra, you're the best for doing this," the boy said.

"Hey, you saved me from those bloody hounds enough times. You deserve it, kid."

He laughed and said, "But that's what brothers and sisters are meant to do for each other."

I said, "We're not brother and sister."

"I know," he said, placing his gloved hands gently on my cheeks, "but if I did have a sister, I'd want her to be just like you."

I had to swallow back a sob, and before I had a chance to reply, he hugged me.

I let one tear roll down my cheek, then gently pushed him away, "You're a good kid, you know," I said screwing on the helmet. "Let's get you into the sunshine."

The memory was a treasured one, and finding those gloves was like a kick to the guts. I started to cry when I saw the broken hover-board fall over within the refrigerator. The fact he'd held onto something so old, something that didn't even work it was just so innocently sweet. It was all a reminder of what I'd lost. What Vic had lost. What the whole world had lost, for that matter.

The last thing I pulled out was the three books. I flicked through them. The first was a book of old myths and legend, fairy tales really. The bedtime stories you're told as a kid by your parents. I had one similar too. The second was called 'My First Book about Engineering.' I smiled, and my heart filled with longing—

this kid. The last book brought back memories of something he said when he got out of the rocket after landing.

"Cyra, Cyra!" he said, bouncing around in his seat still, "I saw one."

"A cloud?"

"No. I mean, yes," he said, both shaking and nodding his head inside the helmet, "I saw loads of clouds. But I mean, I saw a sky whale."

"A what?"

"A sky whale," he said as I led him out of the craft. "They're meant to be extin-" he started and was cut off by a coughing fit, one that lasted for at least five minutes. He stumbled to the ground. Vic sat him up and I put his head between his legs, letting him get his breath back. I forgot to ask more about what he saw. I guess he forgot to tell me, as once he'd composed himself again, all he could talk about was how blue the sky was, how he'd never seen a colour quite so vivid, about how beautiful the sun was, that it was so bright he couldn't even really look at it at all. He was a complete ball of energy after that coughing fit; in fact, he barely coughed at all after for a good few hours, not even to clear his throat. It had me wondering if sunlight could be a natural therapeutic.

Things went crazy after that, and I guess it completely left my mind until that very point. I was looking at a book titled 'Extinct! - 101 Forgotten Beasts That Once Roamed the Earth'. It was another kid's book, full of illustrations. Pictures of animals great and small that had apparently roamed the earth in a bygone age. Pictures of sabre-toothed bears, butterflies the size of hovercars, a creature that prowled the oceans with wings, and a face full of tentacles. Then there it was—the Sky Whale.

The drawing of the beast covered the two-page spread. It was a deep cobalt blue colour. At its hind, it had four short, stumpy fins protruding out to the four points of a compass, with a long thin tail undulating in the wind behind. The face was made up of two tiny black eyes, with an ever-gaping mouth that was nearly the same size as the whole of its huge head, lined with millions upon millions of hairs. I read the short blurb below the picture. It read:

The Sky Whale (cete caelo) died out a mere two hundred years ago, hunted to extinction by man. Each Sky Whale stayed aloft thanks to the gas that filled its body. It's for this gas that the humans hunted the Sky Whale and the gas's uses in industry. The Sky Whale fed on the atmosphere, thanks to the very fine hairs coating its mouth the Sky Whale constantly feeds as it flies through the sky, using millions of tiny bristles along its skin to propel it. It takes in and actively feeds on the many harmful ozone gases, then excretes crisp, clean air, high in oxygen. While its extinction isn't confirmed, no sightings of the creature have been made in over two hundred years, and that's why this majestic creature made it into the number 74 spot.

Holy shit, I thought. I've been coming at this the wrong way this whole time. It's not science that's gonna save this world, it's nature. It's the Sky Whale, and the kid saw one.

I closed the book and then came that first, ominous cough.

The clock was ticking then; I could have a matter of weeks or, if I was lucky, a year of good health. Either way, I made a plan there and then in my head. I'd travel to Cell City, to the Cell City Central Library. I'd find more books on this creature, learn its habits and figure out exactly where this thing could be. I'd find it, and somehow, I'd bring it back here, let it feed on the Smog. Bring back the sunshine. Then with the Smog gone, The Bronch would go with it. I'd save the world. With one problem out the way, I'd then turn my mind to the vampires. That wasn't all that long ago, and I wonder how I could have been so naïve.

I packed a bag—my wind-up flashlight, some food and water, a compass, change of clothes, and a few tools too, you never know when they'll come in handy—and was ready to go the next morning.

"You should take Ace with you," Vic said, "it'll protect you on your travels. Word is Cell City is a hell hole now."

"No. You keep Ace, Vic," I said. "I'll be able to travel faster and quieter alone. I'll keep to the shadows, be careful."

Vic shook his head and stroked his now greying beard; he knew how thick-headed I was, knew that once my mind was made up, there was no changing it. It's why he didn't object to me leaving in the first place.

"Here," he said, "take these." He held out the kid's gloves. I'd given him everything I'd found in the refrigerator. He found some drawings and notes in the books, and now the hoverboard sat at the foot of his rocking chair, his feet resting where the kids would've. It was the happiest he'd been in a long time.

I knew it would hurt his feeling declining such a touching present, so I took them and put them in my pack.

"Thanks, Vic."

"No worries."

"No. Thanks for everything. Thanks for taking me in, thanks for keeping me safe, and feeding me and... just thanks for everything."

"You know what, I thought I'd done with being a dad, but when you came along, it gave me a reason to carry on: responsibility. So, thank you. Imma miss you." Then Vic hugged me for the first and only time. His big arms wrapped around me, warm and safe. It felt like when my own dad used to hug me, and I hugged him back tightly. We saved each other; for that time, those ten years, we were exactly what each other needed. We kept each other going.

"I'll be back," I said, knowing I wouldn't be. I was worried about what he might do after

I left, but I had to go, nevertheless.
  "See ya, kid."

Chapter 6

The walk was arduous and lonely. I was used to having someone to talk to, used to the noise of the dump. Out here in the mist and the murk of the world outside the dump, all was silent, save for the odd call of a bird, the occasional bleat from a deer or cry of a wolf off in the distance. They were the worst for me. Every howl sent a shiver down my back and brought back memories of the night my parents died. Brought back fresher memories of the howls me and Vic heard just outside the dump in the dead of night. I wondered if the Howler knew I was in the dump. I wondered if he was watching, waiting for his chance at revenge. Well, if he was out there, now was the time to get me.

No one came, though, and I trudged onward to Cell City, past abandoned houses, neglected farms, and dilapidated storefronts, seeing neither human nor vampire.

I was getting within a few miles of Cell City when I saw my first chicken in ten years. I was looking through the gloom up toward the skyline of where Cell City would be. It was said that on a good day, even through the Smog, you could see the huge golden globe that sat atop the tallest building in the city. The Precinct, the headquarters of the Cell City Police Department, in better times, it was a symbol of good and justice; a superstition said that it was a good omen should you see the golden globe when entering the city.

As I squinted through the Smog in hopes of catching a glimpse of the globe, I nearly jumped out of my skin; such was the surprise when a chicken came bolting through the Smog, clucking as it went and crashed right into me.

Chickens were never the brightest animal,

and by the time I managed to compose myself, I was able to snag the fowl. Who needed the luck of seeing the golden globe of The Precinct when a bloody chicken lands in your lap?

"Oh, my God!" came a shocked voice through the gloom.

I looked around to see an old lady ten yards away from me. She was easily 70, with short-cropped hair, like she'd chopped at it herself. Her clothes were patched and worn, and she looked thin, but not frail. All things considered, she looked to be doing okay in the circumstances.

"Please," she croaked, "Rosie's all I have."

"Wha... I... it ran straight into me," I spluttered, too surprised at seeing another human being to get much more out.

The old lady held out her hands, showing they were empty. "I mean you no harm. Please, I can offer you food, a bed for the night, just let me have Rosie back."

"Rosie?" I looked at the chicken, and she cooed away happily in my arms. "Oh, the chicken." The red chicken looked to be well fed, and in good health; it was better looked after than the lady. Anyone who would put an animal first was okay in my books. She was so old, I thought I'd be safe around her, and if she did try any funny business, I'd easily be able to fight her off. The day was drawing in, my stomach rumbled, and my feet ached. "I mean you no harm either. I'm just travelling through, to Cell City."

"Hell City, they call it now," she said, waving at me to follow her, "come on. Let's get inside before any unsavouries come."

I followed her through the murk, and we came to a little farmhouse. The windows and doors were boarded up out front, and she led me around back, past a small, well-tended vegetable patch and hand water pump, to a chicken coup, its door was ajar. The lady held it open, and I threw Rosie back in her pen.

"She does that all the time, it's a miracle I've not lost her," The old lady said to me, and cackled, "but I love the stupid ball of fluff, and she keeps me feed. So, I can't complain too much. Come on."

She led me through the backdoor of the house and into a kitchen.

The place was sparse. Not much more than a kitchen table and few seats. The cup-

board doors hung askew or were completely missing, showing off empty shelves. It did
have a wood-burning stove, which warmed the
room nicely, though. It was also secure, the old
lady took off her mask, and I did likewise. I
still wore the mask, you see, people would look
at me differently if I took it off. They'd know I
had The Bronch. Some people, idiots, thought
it was contagious, and God knows what those
sorts of people would do to me. Besides, I was
still in the early stages; the coughing was only
occasional, and luckily the exertion wasn't
yet taking its toll. I dropped the mask into one
of my many coat pockets. I wore a big mili-
tary-style coat. It kept me warm and was good
for carrying all sorts of shit. I took my backpack off my shoulders, placed it on the table,
then removed my coat and hung it across the
back of the chair.

"Please, take a seat," the lady said, "I
don't have much, but can offer you a little food
and a bed for the night."

"Oh, I can't impose on you little that."

"Child, you'll need your rest if you're
heading into the city."

I was tired, and a night's rest in a comfy bed sure sounded better than camping out in some abandoned building, so I agreed and thanked her.

"Some tea?"

"Tea?" I said shocked, I hadn't had tea in forever. "Yes, please, miss. I'd love a cup."

The old lady cackled as my eyes must have bulged clear out of their sockets. "Please, call me Jo. And let me tell ya, it'll be as weak as cat's piss. It's been brewed within an inch of its life."

This time it was my turn to laugh, "I'll take it," I said, taking a seat, "Thanks so much. I'm Cyra."

A small stove-top kettle sat next to the oven; the old lady moved it onto one of the hobs and stood stooping over the oven, warming her hands. Soon, steam whistled from the kettle, and Jo poured two cups of tea. No milk, though.

"Here you go, Cyra. What a lovely name," Jo said and placed two chipped metal camping mugs on the table. "Why on earth are you on your way to Hell City?"

"I'm headed for the library," I said, leaving it at that. I didn't want to talk too much about my plan; I didn't want to give it too much hope just yet. I sipped at the tea—it was weak, but it was warm and tasted amazing, the first tea I'd had in years—and asked, "I'm more worried about why they call it Hell City now?"

"Well, deary, the vampires have set up shop there. They run the place now. I've had a few travellers, like yourself, come through these parts, heading for the city. None of 'em come back, though."

A hollow, sick feeling in my stomach overtook me. I knew the trip would be danger-ous but had no idea I'd be going into a hornet's nest. "Are there any safe routes in?"

"There may be one," Jo said, "but first, can I interest you in a little dinner? It's best to talk of these things on a full stomach, I find."

"I couldn't, Jo," I said, looking toward the empty cupboards.

"Oh, nonsense. I wouldn't offer if I didn't have enough to spare. Go on out to Rosie's pen; there should be a couple of eggs in there we can have with a little flatbread I have."

A fresh egg. I can't convey quite how ex-citing the idea of a fresh egg was. My mouth filled with saliva. Just the thought of breaking a runny yoke over some bread was heavenly. I popped my coat back on, grabbed my backpack off the table, and slung it on my back. Jo seemed nice enough, but you could never be sure.

My mask was back on as I walked out the kitchen door and out into the blanket of Smog as the day was beginning to darken. I walked to the chicken coup, where I could hear Rosie clucking away happily. I opened the coup door and walked in; Rosie trotted over and began idly pecking at my shoelaces. Carefully, I walked past her and lifted the roof on her little house. Nestled within fresh straw were a couple of fresh eggs, still sporting the odd feather courtesy of Rosie. I gently picked them both out and closed the lid.

"Thank you, Rosie," I said, "thank you, thank you, thank you!"

As the lid to Rosie's home locked back down, I noticed a shed just through the gloom. It was a massive shed, very much like my workshop back home, stood with its doors open, revealing a car. An honest to goodness car, not a hovercar, no no, an actual, antique, four-wheeled car. Even covered in dust, its chrome bumper shone in what was left of the light; it was a beauty. I walked up and down the flank taking it all in; I wondered if it still ran. Even if it didn't, what I would give to work on this car, to learn its ticks. To drive it! But it was just a dream, time was running out, and I couldn't spend the day, or even weeks on something like this, even though I wanted to.

As I rounded the car, about to take a closer look at its rear, I spotted a treasure trove. I hadn't noticed before, because of the car, but this shed was full of boxes—all overflowing with great stuff. The kinds of things I drooled to get my hands on back in my shop. The first one I looked at was a box of batteries. Not the usual run of the mill batteries, but big, what we called, baked bean batteries. They were the batteries we used for our guard dogs at the dump; they just happened to be the size and shape of a tin of baked beans. I gently placed the eggs in one of my few empty pockets and then pulled a battery from the box and looked it over; it looked to be pretty much brand new. Luckily, I'd packed the universal tester, so I quickly whipped it out of my bag and gave it a go. It buzzed with life. A broad smile crossed my face, and I popped it in my bag, after glancing around and making sure I wasn't being watched.

I'm not really sure why I just took it, as I'm not a thief. I guess the fact that there was a box full, I figured Jo wouldn't miss just one.

After my bag was back on my shoulders, I opened up another box nearby, this one was full of dog jaw bones. Not actual dogs. The robotic ones. One of the great things with the guard dogs is that you could change their bottoms jaws should you need them for anything else. Ours were mostly just used as guard dogs, but there were so many different jaws available. Crushers and shredders, mulchers and magnets. To name a few. This box was full of magnetic jaws. They each had an incredibly strong electromagnet embedded in them, which would be used to help sort through random scrap in the yard, pulling out all the metal. There were tens in this box, so I also pocketed one of those, thinking, if I do ever go past the dump again, I'd drop these off to Vic, who would undoubtedly find uses for them.

I zipped my bag up, putting it back over my shoulders, not a minute too soon. A coughing fit overtook, one that came from deep in my lungs. It was my first coughing fit of the day, and it was a doozy. I stood doubled over, hand on the boot of the car, this close to being sick, thanks to the severity of the cough. Luckily, it subsided before it got to that. When I stood back up, Jo was looking down at me with eyes full of horror, the rest of her face didn't show it, but her eyes did for a moment before the look just became sad and knowing.

"How long?" she simply asked.

I wiped the cough induced tears from my eyes and offered a weak smile. "Had my first cough a couple of days ago. It's not contagious." I offered, hoping to alleviate any lasting fears she may have had.

"I know," she purred and gave me the saddest smile I've ever seen. She may as well have come out and said, 'sorry you're dying, kiddo'.

I didn't want her pity; I was well aware of what was happening to me. So, I turned to the car instead and spread my arms wide.

"You've found The Beast, I see."

"Beast?!" I cried, "This is a thing of beauty."

"That she is, that she is," Jo said, and that

was that. My case of The Bronch seemed to be forgotten.

"Does she run?"

"No engine in her," Jo said and waved around the shed to all the boxes, "there's everything needed to build one in here somewhere, but it's fit to topple down like dominos before I could find them. Come on, let's get inside before we're buried alive in here."

Disappointed, I followed Jo out, taking a last glance at the car as she shut the doors behind us.

"You get those eggs?"

"Yeah, got them right here," I said, pulling the pair out of my pocket.

"Good girl. Let's get cooking."

***

We had a modest dinner consisting of our egg, each topping a small flatbread. A pile of the ever-present mushrooms was on the side, next to a few greens. Chard. The veg I knew best. It brought home a pang of loss. I hadn't eaten chard in a while either, and as we ate in silence, I found myself thinking of everything that was lost. My parents, wondering what they would make of the world as it was. Society. Now Vic and the dump. And, of course, as always, the boy.

Jo brought me out of my melancholy memories, when she said with a sigh, "Well, I guess we better talk then."

I gave her a weak smile, showing my consent. It was near full dark now and Jo walked around lowering all of the lamps, so we had not much more than a whisper of light. "Can't advertise to the vampires that we're here," she said.

Finally, when the lights were sufficiently dimmed, and she was good and ready, Jo said, "The city ain't no place for a girl, no more, a human girl anyway. They don't call it Hell City for nothing."

"I have to go," I said, simply.

"Okay, well, I can see you're not going to give me much more in the way of details," she paused. I remained silent. "And there's no talking you out of going?" I simply shook my head. She looked down and slowly shook her head. It was one that reminded me of Vic, but her's had more look of defeat in it. A knowing. One that said, she knew she wouldn't ever be

57

seeing me again. "Ok, then."

She then went on to describe a way into the city which she'd heard was relatively safe, and that she'd draw me a map, ready to go the next morning.

We had one last cup of tea and shared some small talk, and then she showed me to her spare room, leading the way up the rickety stairs with one small oil lamp.

The room was already made up. A simple single bed, with one pillow and a duvet drawn down, inviting me in. A few blankets lied at the end of the bed, too, should I need them.

"Well, Cyra," Jo said, "thank you for your company tonight. I don't get too many visitors this way anymore, but I wish there were more I could do for you."

"No, thank you, Jo," I said. "You've already done more than enough. I wish there were a way I could repay you. Maybe I'll bring you something back from the city."

She smiled at me, but her eyes were as empty as the wastelands I'd been walking all day. "I'd like that," was what she said, but her face was saying, 'I'll never see you alive again.'. "If you need anything, holla. I'm just down the hall on the left."

"Thanks again, Jo."

She left the room, shutting the door as she went. I sat on the bed, dumping my bag next to me. It was lumpy, but it was a bed, and I was asleep, fully clothed, before I knew what hit me.

Chapter 7

At first, I thought I was having a nightmare. I'd dreamt of that night many times. The blood, the screaming, the flames, and of course, the howling. As I stirred on the lumpy bed, my backpack being used as a pillow, I thought I was just having another nightmare. The howling came from all around, getting louder and louder.

Pounding footsteps came rumbling up the stairs, and I sprang up. Fully awake in an instant and looking around the dark room confused.

The howls surrounded the house and grew

louder as the intruders came upstairs. The old lady. Jo, I thought, we're in danger. I grabbed my bag, and as soon as I did, the howling ceased outside the door.

I sat, goosebumps rose all over my body, and I felt a shiver run down my back. Looking at the door I heard a slight squeak as the door handle was turned. I jumped into action, dropping my backpack. I ran to block the door, but I was too late. By the time I reached the door whoever was behind it had the momentum. I tried pushing the door shut, but my clammy hands just slipped off. The door whipped open, clonking me in the head. Stars erupted in my head, and I stumbled backward.

Through blurred vision, I saw two men enter the room, one holding a lit torch. Then the howling began all over again, between the cries and excited hollers of the two vampires.

"We have one!"

"Fresh as a daisy!"

One vampire grabbed me by the hair, pulling my head back. I felt his breath on my neck as he sniffed me like I was a piece of steak just off the barbecue. I guess to that monster, I was. Then I felt a warm, sticky tongue run its way up my neck, and despite my fight to hold onto consciousness, I felt revulsion deep in the pit of my stomach and tried to fight back.

I stamped on the vampire's foot, he screamed out in surprise. A second later, before he could recover, I swung an elbow toward his face. I heard the sickening crunch as his nose broke beneath the thick bone of my elbow and felt an immediate elation. He lost his grip on me, no doubt fumbling at his face, and I took off trying to make a run for it.

I got no further than the bedroom door when the second vampire threw a solid punch directly at my chest. It felt like my lungs leapt into my mouth as I keeled over, unable to breathe.

"Would you stop playing around? We have a job to do, you fool," the man with the torch said. "Get up off that dirty floor and take her downstairs."

"Da bitz bwoke my dose," the other one mumbled through blood and tears.

"Quickly now," the other hissed.

The vampire with the broken nose grabbed me by the arm and ripped me off the floor, pushing me out of the bedroom, and started to lead me downstairs. Through tears and dizziness, I saw a bevy of vampires surrounding Jo.

"I'm sorry," she cried. "I didn't know."

"The only reason we keep you alive, living the high life like this, is to get us, good, clean," the man said that word with real emphasis, "stock. What do we not want?"

"I'm sorry, I didn't realise until after I'd called you. I thought she was clean. The case is only new, so maybe she'll still be okay." Jo pleaded.

What was she saying? I remember wondering.

"I'll repeat, Jo. What. Do. We. Not. Want?"

"You don't want people with The Bronch."

"Well done, Jo. So, you do know the rules, and yet you chose to ignore them and get us all out here in the dead of night, for a dud."

"I'm sorry, I'm sorry. Please. Just please let me stay, and I'll get you more; lots more. Everyone will be clean and delicious. It'll never happen again." Jo cried.

My vision was starting to clear now, as I stood on the last step watching over the proceedings. Jo had got down onto her hands and knees and was crying, begging for mercy with the vampire who was obviously in charge here. Unlike the vampires I saw that fateful night all those years ago, these were well dressed, the vampire Jo was now cowering to wore a tailored suit which cried authority.

"You're right, Jo; it won't happen again."

Then the vampire pulled a blade from a sheath behind his back. It was short and shined razor-sharp. The blade sang as he swept it through the air and through Jo's neck. Blood sprayed him like a shower. The silver eyes of all the vampires went wide, shining bright in the dark room. "Dinner is served."

Recognition hit like a wave. The vampire turned to me, revealing the dark, hollow socket where an eye had once resided. It was One-eye.

Chapter 8

I woke up in the back of a pick-up truck as it hovered above the cracked blacktop that was now ribboned with vegetation. It was still dark, and the Smog seemed thicker than usual; the headlights made it looked as if we were swimming through smoke.

We were close to the city; I could see the lights on, reaching far up into the sky. They all came from the same place, and although I couldn't see the building yet, I knew it was The Precinct.

"Ah, you're awake," Henry said. "Welcome back."

I sneered at him, not making a sound. It was just the two of us in the back of the pick-up.

"How's your head?" he tried.

My hand went to the back of my head; it was throbbing in time to my heartbeat. I had a lump the size of a golf ball there. I thought back to the last thing I could remember. The look of recognition that came over One-eye's one eye, back in the house. A look of shock and then of evil happiness.

"You," One-eye said, all too knowingly.

I broke the vampire's grip behind me and ran for him, I had no idea what I was doing, but I knew I wanted him dead. He'd murdered my mum, drank her blood, for fucks sake. I'd often dreamt of meeting him again and killing him and now was my chance. Before I could get to him, though, another vampire caught me around the waist. He was a lot younger than the rest, a couple of years older than me, maybe. He had short blonde hair, and despite being a vampire, a kind face. It was all ruined by the metal-silver eyes, though.

"I'll fucking kill you," I screamed, trying to fight my way through.

"Don wowwy bozz, I'll kill thhith bitz," said the vampire whose nose I'd just broke.

"You'll do no such thing," One-eye said. "Charles will be wanting a chat with this little chicken."

"This is her?" The young vampire said.

"Yes, Henry. It is."

I spat in One-eye's direction. "Fuck you."

"You should be thanking me, you know. Any other human with The Bronch would just be slaughtered, like Jo here. It's lucky I remembered. Charles will be wanting a word with you. And so would I for that matter," he said, raising a hand to his empty eye socket. "And by word, of course, I mean some light torture, no doubt."

I kicked and fought to get at him, and then I heard a hollow pop at the back of my head; it was the last thing I could remember.

"My head kills," I said to Henry, the young vampire. "What are they gonna do with me?"

"I'm honestly, not sure. I'm kind of new to this. Here, have a drink," he said, holding out a bottle of water.

I sniggered but took the water and gulped down a few mouthfuls. "Don't need this, I guess," I said taking off my mask and throwing away. "Guessing you lot can't catch The Bronch then? Why can't you eat us?"

He looked a little confused and sad all at once, like he wasn't quite sure how to answer the question. "No, I don't think we-"

"Henry! Keep it quiet back there." One-eye shouted from upfront.

"Sorry," Henry whispered.

The rest of the journey was completed in silence. The pick-up hummed through the city; an echo played back off the empty buildings, giving the place an eerie vibe. The Precinct neared, and soon we entered its garage on the bottom level. The pick-up was parked in one of the empty bays, and we all shuffled out.

As I exited the pick-up, I looked around, surprised to see around a third of the electric lights were shining. They'd been replaced with low-voltage, energy-saving bulbs, which cast a dull glow across the whole garage. It told me that the vampires were organised and knowledgeable enough to keep generators or some sort of renewable energy source going. This building was more than a simple lair; keeping the electricity going after all this time told me this place was very important. Most of the parking spots were empty, like the majority of the garage, but at the opposite end were two large transport hover-trucks.

A line of people were passing crates of something from one to the next, loading them into the trucks. I squinted, trying to make out what was in the crates.

I thought of making a run for it, but before my two feet were on the floor, One-eye grabbed my upper arm, squeezing far tighter than was necessary. I bit my lip to suppress a cry; I wouldn't give them the satisfaction.

"Thank you, Henry. Run along ahead and ready our guest here a cell."

"Yes, Giles," he said.

Henry ran off ahead, shooting a concerned look back in my direction for just a second, as Giles began to lead me into the building.

"Welcome to The Precinct," he said, through a smirk. "You'll see some real wonders here."

I said nothing.

"You know, I've often wondered what we would do to you should we ever cross paths again. Charles has spoken at length about the horrors he wants to inflict on you, but I don't want to spoil the surprise. I almost feel sorry for you; I, for one, don't hold much of a grudge against you personally. I mean, it was your witch of a mother who gouged my eye out, not you."

I turned on him in an instant and went for his last good eye, trying to claw to out.

A look of shock flashed across his face, but he was too big and too strong. A back-hand whipped across my face, sending me sprawling. My cheek felt like fire, but through gritted teeth, I managed to say, "Don't you ever talk about my mother."

He actually smiled at me, "You have some fight in you; I'll give you that. Let's see how long that lasts."

I was led to a staircase, and we started to climb. Up and up, floor after floor, we climbed. We must have climbed a thousand steps. My calves burned, and I collapsed a couple of times when they cramped up. The vampires showed me no mercy and just kicked me until I got up and carried on. Eventually, we made it to the floor I was destined to live on—the 111th.

As we came to 111th floor landing we

heard a groan. It got louder and louder until it was on the other side of the door we were facing.

"Welcome to hell," Giles said smugly and swung the doors open onto a sight of pure horror. This was hell on earth.

The smell hit me first. The overwhelming scent of sickness that sat next to the eye-stinging aroma of human waste and was topped by a metallic aftertaste.

A woman lay on a bed groaning softly. No, that's too kind a description. It was little more than a metal cot covered by a thin mattress. She might have been thirty or sixty by the looks of her. Her head had been shaved bald, and her eyes looked sunken next to the thin trails of tears. Although not emancipated, she was thin, having very little in the way of muscle definition. She'd been there for a long time. She was tied to the bed at the wrists and ankles by leather straps. Sores and welts were clear to see where the shackles rubbed. A line drew out of her arm, attached to a cannula. Blood was being let out of the woman and collected in what looked like a glass coke bottle next to the bed.

Identical beds ran up and down the football pitch sized room, rows and rows of them—each with a man, woman or child in. Each being bled.

I hesitate to call them this, but vampiric nurses walked the rows, switching off the cannula's, collecting the bottles of steaming blood and putting them into crates on trollies. This is what they'd been loading into the truck, blood. Human, fucking blood. It made me nauseous.

All the while, other vampires circulated, sticking feeding tubes down people's throats and injecting something that looked like porridge. Furthermore, a third group was also on-site, swapping out buckets that sat under the bed, collecting human waste.

I have and will never see another scene as barbaric as that; my stomach lurched as Giles finished the scene for me, "This is just one of many like floors here. We like to call them The Herd."

I doubled over and vomited up what little dinner I had left in my stomach.

Chapter 9

My cell was a small dark room, probably used to be an office in better times. There was a large window, not that I could see anything out of it, apart from the dull, monotonous grey of the Smog. I had the same metal cot, the same thin mattress, and the same bucket for shitting in. Thank God, no shackles for me, though. The smell and the groans never left, they both somehow wafted through the walls to me, but thankfully, I couldn't see all the poor, helpless people in the room—but I would, all too much. There was one silver lining to this room though. Something of a small miracle, all things considered. A corpse lay in the corner of the room. How it got there and why I have never found out, but to my amazement, our lost robot guard dog, Bowser, laid dormant in the corner. His lower jaw and baked bean battery were missing, but his clipped ear was clear to see. It was definitely Bowser. At that moment he was just a lump of metal, was someone to talk to and bounce ideas off of, but if I had a couple of parts, I could get him working again. It wasn't much, but it was a little hope—the bud of an idea and something that kept me sane in the weeks that followed.

It took three days before Charles paid me a visit.

I heard the howling first, of course. Charles, previously known as The Howler, was coming my way. Fear shot through my bones, my hands started to shake, and I clasped them together, willing them to stop. I sat up on my bed and resolved myself to show no fear. The ceiling lights illuminated the room for the first and only time during my stay.

"Well, well, well," I heard as the door opened and Charles entered. "Here she finally is. Rocketgirl!"

I looked to Charles, unlike the last time I saw him, he too, now wore the finery of a distinguished gentleman. The pin-stripe navy suit and brown leather shoes did nothing to hide the raw, red scars on the left side of his face, the cloudy, white eye, and the missing ear. I didn't feel shame for the injuries I'd caused, and I didn't feel pride either. All I felt looking at this man was regret. Regret I hadn't killed him. Regret he was still alive. And regret at what he did to me.

I bit my tongue; I knew I had to hold myself back then. I had no way of getting to him and killing him then. I had to use my intellect. I had to learn everything I could, and I had to build something, just like the machines I used to build; I had to draw up the blueprints of a plan, build, and then I'd get my revenge. Finding the Sky Whales, saving the world, was a distant memory.

"You want to kill me, don't you?" Charles said and chuckled, "I can see the rage in your eyes. I wanted to kill you once upon a time too, you know. Just after you did this to me," he said and ran a hand down his mottled cheek.

"Why haven't you then? You're a monster. That's what monsters do."

"Come now, let's be civil. Call me Charles, Cyra," he said with a smirk like I should be shocked that he would know my name.

"You're not clever; I know Jo told you-" I started but was cut off with a cough.

"You're a clever one, aren't you? Well, we'll get that out of you soon enough. To answer your question, why would I kill you now? You're already dying; that would be too easy. I'm going to prolong this, put you through hell before killing you. You still need to pay for what you did to me."

"What I did to you!" I shouted in rage. "What I did to you? And what about what you and your thugs did to my parents? Murdered them in cold blood! Sliced them open in front of me, drank-" I broke down there and cried, I couldn't finish, my rage was all used up.

"Well, for the method and circumstances of their death, I do apologise. We were all in the throes of madness that night. We'd yet to reclaim our civility."

"Civility?" I croaked. "You call this civility."

"You humans are now what cows were

to us all. You're all just farmed food. Fed and milked for what we need."

"Not me, though. Does The Bronch not agree with your vampiric digestion?" I started to probe.

"Ahh, The Bronch." He said, almost wistful. "The cause of all this. No, we cannot feed on victims of The Bronch. Well, we can when needs are most dire, but it doesn't agree with them, hence why we set up The Herd. A safe space, away from the Smog and risk of infection. Clean stock is a rare commodity now."

Them? Why The Bronch? I thought, but before I had the chance to dig any further, a lackey stepped in and whispered in his ear.

"Well, Cyra, I must leave you for now. But fear not, I'll be back at some point, so look forward to that. I have a feeling our next meeting won't be quite so civil. But, while you're waiting, I've assigned you a job. You get to clean out all of your friends' shit buckets. Enjoy." His face contorted in what was meant to be a smile but was just plain psychotic. Then he howled once more, making me jump.

***

Days were spent wandering the rows of beds, switching out buckets of shit and piss for empty buckets. Every man, woman, and child groaned, so weak they could barely move, but each of them, at one point, saw me, recognised me as one of their own, and even in their poor state of health were able to give me a look of contempt. On one occasion, a small child of indiscriminate sex grabbed my arm; I looked down and just for a second saw the boy lying there.

"Please, help me," he croaked.

I could only pull my arm away and run.

My nights, although I barely had the strength too, I looked at my situation, at all of the data I had, trying to come up with some plan. My goals had shifted again; I needed to save these people. If I could give one boy sunshine, I could figure out a way to give these people their freedom. I had to; there was simply no one else who would. It was hard to think though, at least once a week, Charles would come past howling. I'd awake, terrified at what he might do to me. I realise now that he was torturing me. My body was already breaking down, and now he was breaking me down mentally, piece by piece.

My cough got worse and worse as the weeks went by. Henry brought me food twice a day, morning and night, the same gruel they force-fed the rows of people on. It was tasteless, slimy, and gag-inducing, but I ate every scrap. I needed my strength.

Henry, at least, was what could pass as nice for a vampire. When he'd drop off my food, we'd speak occasionally. Not about my situation, or the vampires or the Smog or The Bronch, but about life that used to be. We spoke about our hobbies, our favourite foods, and our old friends. We maybe even became friends.

One evening I summoned up the courage to ask him, "Why are you here? Why do you help them? You're not like the others."

He looked to me, forlorn. "I hate myself," he started. "I hate what I am, but I have no choice. They caught me, just like they caught you. There are people and places like Jo and the farm all over. Each, a recruitment station, they call them. Ready to pounce on any travellers healthy enough to join The Herd."

He shook his head and looked away wistfully, clearly remembering the day. "It wasn't long before we got you. I came upon a place similar to where you ended up, tricked into spending the night, and then jumped upon by a group of vampires. I was with some friends; three of us were just doing what we could to survive. They're in The Herd now. An advisor to Charles, Giles sister, in fact, took a liking to me. She gave me an ultimatum, join The Herd, or be her little pet. She made me drink her blood and become one of them. I wish I'd joined The Herd. I wish I was fucking dead." Henry broke down, crying then. Tears flecked with silver ran down his cheeks, twinkling in the dull light. "They make me drink my friends' blood now. I hate them; I hate myself."

This was my chance; Charles wouldn't wait forever; it was now or never. I gave Henry a minute before asking, "What if I had a way to get out of here? Get us both out and away."

He choked and laughed through the tears. "And how are you going to do that?" he asked, humouring me.

"Back at the house, where you found me. I had a bag; in it, I had stashed a baked bean battery and robot guard dog jaw. You get me those, and I'll get this guy working," I said, pointing to Bowser.

"That bag will be long gone, we've got someone else posted out there now."

I pressed on. "That's fine. There's a whole shed full of them out the back. Just grab me one of each."

Henry had doubt plastered all over his face. He looked around the room, to the Bowser, like he was searching for an answer. Finally, he found it, "I can't."

Frustration and fear all welled up and overflowed in an instant, "Why!?" I screamed at him.

"Ssshh," Henry exclaimed, shocked at the outburst. He quickly walked over to the door and stuck his head, looking both ways. Satisfied, he came back. "Do you want them to know I'm talking to you?"

"Sorry," I said, begging now. "Please, you've got to help me. Help us."

Henry looked at me like I was a lost puppy. Like, I just didn't get it. Then a light sparked in his eyes. "You don't know, do you?"

I looked at him blankly.

"You don't know what happened that night, the night the vampires ascended, do you?"

"Does it really matter? It's the zombie apocalypse, but with vampires instead. It doesn't matter if some ancient disease came out of the permafrost, or some comet brought it to earth. We're all fucked, and that's all that really matters."

"What if it does matter, though?" Henry asked and fell silent.

I waited for him to tell me, and waited, "Well, come on! Out with it."

Henry gazed off into the middle distance and gathered his thoughts, "It all starts with the Smog. When that came all those hundreds of years ago, it brought with it a disease. That was the zombie apocalypse moment, but instead of making zombies, it just killed people. Half the world searched for a way to clear the Smog; the other looked for a cure for The Bronch."

"Right, and no solution to either has ever been found."

"Ahh, but it has," Henry said.

"The vampires. You. You're all immune to The Bronch. I asked why you couldn't drink my blood, but never why you're immune."

"You ever wonder why the majority of

vampires are well dressed, well-spoken? Apart from me, and the ones they've turned, that is."

"It had crossed my mind, but I just assumed the clothes had been stolen."

"After trying and failing over and over and over, eventually LexGo Corp and Circe Pharmaceuticals joined forces to try and find a cure. And they did. I have no idea if it was tested properly, but I'm guessing it wasn't. Either way, they had created a cure. A very expensive cure. One that they could only offer to the elite class to start with."

I chuckled, but it quickly escalated into a coughing fit. Once it had passed, I continued, "If you've got money, then you gotta have things first, right?"

"Exactly. For the rich, being able to walk around with no mask on, without fear of catching The Bronch would be a status symbol."

"So, the medicine caused all this?"

"No. Well, yes." Henry stammered. "Sort of."

"The cure to The Bronch, the creation of the vampires was a nano-robotic pill."

"Nano-robots?"

"Yes, these nano-robots actively fight off

infections, including The Bronch. Vampires never get ill, but it turns out they burn through iron like you wouldn't believe. The pills were distributed and activated that night. The night of the slaughter."

"Iron?" I said, mulling it over. "Iron. So, when they were switched on the people, the vampires, they couldn't control the need and hunger of the robots. They needed iron."

"And human blood has a good concentration of iron in it. The nano-robots knew not to go for each other and so they went for those who didn't take the pills. They went for anything with good levels of iron really."

"I saw a herd of cows bleed dry the morning after, and now that I think of it, our chard fields were bare too."

"That night, they wiped out so much," Henry said.

"But we survive. Humans are resilient and we persevered."

"Yes, and now you're the herd, and that's why I can't get those things for you. That whole barn is off-limits for us. Why do you think we have a human down there?"

"The batteries, the magnets," I said, thinking out loud. "They mess with the nano-ro-bots," I whispered. It was all coming together. "They must act as a low-level EMP. Wiping the nano-robots, essentially killing them."

"It hurts like you wouldn't believe. We still need humans to dismantle the guard dogs; if I went into that barn, it would probably kill me."

It all came together then, the plan in my head. Not only would I be able to get out, but I thought I could even save everyone else trapped in here, being sucked dry.

"You need to get me my backpack. That only has one battery in," I said. "It'll hurt, but you can do it."

Henry was silent.

"If not for me, and if not for yourself, do it for your friends in there," I hissed, pointing out the door, "Your friends, who are right now tied on a bed, shitting into a bucket, being force-fed and bleed dry. Do it for all the children out there, do it to save what little humanity you may have left." I implored.

"Okay, okay," Henry said. "I'll try, but as I told you, it will be gone by now."

The next morning Henry came round with

my slurry breakfast confirming my fears; the bag was gone, and with it my hopes.

Then, later that night, the howling came again. This time it stopped outside my door. "See you tomorrow, Cyra." Came the voice of Charles, "Sleep well."

Chapter 10

The day went by in a blur. I felt numb with terror, knowing that Charles would come for me that night, and I would have no way to fight back, no hope of escape.

I emptied the buckets, not feeling the sting of ammonia in my eyes, without seeing my withering cousins on the bed. I didn't smell the shit or feel the regret for their—our—lost lives. I just floated through the day, willing it to both end and not too.

That evening when they threw me back into my cell, I tripped and fell face-first to the ground. The door slammed shut behind me.

and the lock clicked into place. I wanted to just lay there, I wished I'd just fall asleep and never wake up again, but I knew I'd get no such luck and resolved myself to somehow keep going. I peeled my face off of the cold linoleum floor under me, and as I went to get up, I saw my backpack tucked under the bed, and next to it, a bowl of slurry.

I felt too much all at once, happiness, confusion, hope, fear. Henry had come through. Somehow, someway. I didn't know what to do with myself, but I knew I didn't have long. So, after what felt like years, but was in actual fact just a few months, I set to work again. Tools out, building, reaching for sunshine.

This is the part of the movie where you'd see a montage of me inspecting my tools, and Bowser, pulling the new parts from my backpack; you'd see me sweating and building. You'd hear the uplifting music as I created hope from nothing. Then, finally, once the music died, you'd see me smiling, proud of the job I'd finished, then the camera would pan out to reveal the coolest, most arse-kicking robot guard dog on the planet, and then I'd punch the sky.

90

In reality, it took me two seconds. The jaw just clicks into place, and the baked bean battery is as easy as switching out the batteries in your hoverboard.

Bowser came back online. He didn't wag his tail or lick me like a real dog, but when I told him to sit, he did, and that meant he'd follow my commands to the letter. I had a chance. My plan still had a chance, and with some luck, I might be able to save a few of the poor souls in that building.

I told Bowser to go back to where he'd been lying dead in the corner and then waited for the howling to start.

The howling never came, but the clip-clop of shoes came echoing down the hall and into my cell. A courtesy knock came, the lock clicked off and the door opened, revealing Giles. He stood in the doorway wearing a black suit he looked like a pallbearer about to carry a body to its grave. I looked at him, raising an eyebrow, and he smirked. I realised, then, that he'd worn this as a sick joke, and I narrowed my eyes, my rage building. They'd been mentally torturing me for months, and Giles was keeping it up right until the very end.

"It's a sick joke, I know, but sometimes one cannot help themselves," Giles said, a proud smile across his face.

"You like jokes?" I asked.

"On occasions."

"I bet you like knock-knock jokes, right?" I started and continued before he could answer, "Knock-knock. Who's there? Vampire. Vampire who? Vampire come to rip my mother's throat out. Get it. It's funny because it's true."

Giles smile faded a little, "A little low-brow for my liking, I'm afraid. Come now. Let's get this over with."

"Wait! Please. Just one more joke. A real one this time." I said. Giles looked a little annoyed and checked his watch. "Come on; I'll make it quick. With what you sick fucks are about to do to me, I should be able to tell one more joke at least?"

"Hmmm," Giles sighed. "Okay but make it quick."

I coughed, it was a horrible, phlegmy rasp now, and Giles looked down on me with equal parts disgust and pity. Once it had passed, I continued.

"Knock, knock."

"Who's there?"

"Bowser."

"Bowser who?"

"Bowser, kill the vampire."

A look of genuine terror flashed across Giles' face, his metallic eyes darting to Bowser in the corner, then back to me.

I knew I'd got the sick fuck in that instant, and I savoured every millisecond of it. To see that fear in his eyes, the same fear that must have been in my eyes on that night many years ago. The same fear that I saw in my mother's eyes.

Bowser jumped to his feet in an instant and bounded toward Giles. Giles turned to run away, but Bowser was too quick; he'd closed the distance in just a couple of seconds. The click-ping of Bowser's paws echoed in my ears with each footstep he took until there was silence as he leapt into the air aiming straight for Giles' neck. Giles tried to get an arm up in time, but Bowser's new jaw just tore straight through the one finger Giles managed to get up. A cry came from his throat but was quickly silenced as Bowsers jaws clamped down on his neck.

Bowser didn't thrash or shake his head as

you would expect of a real dog. Instead, the instant he clamped down, the electromagnet in his jaw activated.

Giles tried to scream, but all that came out was a stifled squeak. The next couple of seconds were a horror show. Giles stood, attempting to scream and shaking at the same time. His hand shot up first, going for the dog's jaw. Next, he fell to the floor, before his knees shot up to the dog's jaw also, leaving him crouched, looking like he was trying to hug Bowser's snout. The shaking intensified, and as it did so, Giles face and hands went redder and redder until the blood started to flow. I knew at that moment that, what I hoped would happen was happening. Bowser's electromagnetic jaw was strong enough to literally suck all the nano-robots from Giles' body. Blood seeped out of his eyes, his ears, his nose, from under his fingernails, from every pore in his body. The nano-robots ripped through his body and his clothes. By the time his squeaking screaming ceased and he was, finally, blessedly dead, his clothes and body looked like it had been through a shredder.

I didn't have time to feel remorse; that

would come later. He was, after all, still a human—a deeply disturbed human, but human none the less.

"Bowser, come," I said, heading for the door after grabbing my backpack.

Bowser immediately dropped the limp mangled body, and it collapsed to the floor, lifeless. I walked down the hall, a featureless, dimly lit tunnel leading to more office-come-cells, and finally before the stairs and the exit out, the room that held The Herd. I could hear the tap of Bowsers claws over their groans and vowed to them that I'd be back.

I reached the end of the hall and glanced into the room full of captive people and couldn't have timed it worse. A vampire nurse was bleeding the man on the end of the row and looked me dead in the eyes; her silver, mechanical eyes brightened in confusion. I didn't give her the time to shout, and I didn't set Bowser on her; that would have just made more of a commotion alerting everyone to my escape. Instead, I took off down the stairs.

I went as quickly as I could, two, three steps at a go. When I hit the 100th floor, an alarm started, no doubt raised by the nurse who spotted me. It was a high-pitched intermittent whir, screeching out my escape; in my ears, it sounded like a witch screaming 'DIIIIIE-DIIIIIE - DIIIIIE over and over. My body tensed, and I expected a flood of vampires to converge on me from above and below. They never came.

Getting down the stairs was certainly easier, than going up, but my problem was The Bronch. By the time I hit the 65th floor, my lungs were starting to cry out for more air, and I was coughing every couple of floors I descended. The Bronch was stealing my lungs, bit by bit. I had to press on though; I had to get out. Bowser followed every step I took, I knew he could have bounded down all 111 floors in half the time it took me to get halfway down, but Bowser followed my every command and stayed with me.

When I came to the 13th floor, I was wheezing heavily, and I felt like I might pass out. I got to the landing and had to rest; I'd come down nearly 100 floors, my feet ached, and my body felt like it had been thrown in a tumble dryer for an hour. I hunched over, my hand on my knees trying to catch my breath when the door to the floor swung open, and a confused-looking vampire bumped into me, nearly knocking me down the rest of the stairs.

"Terribly sorry," he said, and I even managed to marvel at the fact there was a polite vampire. "What's going on?" he asked, then, "Oh shit."

He must have seen Bowser.

"Ill im." I croaked.

Bowser just stood by my side.

I looked up to see those characteristic silver eyes looking down at me. A confused look quickly went to one of anger and then indecision. I knew he wasn't sure what to do; try to grab me or run and get help. Instead, he just froze, doing nothing, mouth agape.

I coughed once, clearing my throat. I was taking no chances. "Kill him," I said, clear this time.

Bowser leapt into action, and soon, there was a bloody mess on the landing.

I took a deep breath, the short rest allowing me to gain some composure, and carried on down the stairs. I heard multiple shouts from above. They'd taken longer than I could ever have imagined or hoped for, but now the chase was on.

When I finally hit the ground floor, I came out in the garage where I had arrived. Standing there, waiting for me, were five vampires, four men, and a woman. I didn't recognise them but wondered if the woman was Giles sister, the one who'd turned Henry. Judging by the look of sheer hate on her face, I thought it likely.

"Come quietly, you fucking bitch," she said, "and I'll make it quick."

By now, I could barely breathe; my throat felt like it was closing up, and my vision was narrowing. I had to move now, or it would all be over, so I took one deep wheezing breath and said, "Bowser, kill her."

Again, Bowser followed my command and went straight for the woman. The other vampires looked on in terror as blood bloomed all over her body, sucking out the nano-robots, making her a mangled, bloody mess, and killing her all at the same time. They all began to back off them, wanting to keep as much distance between themselves and Bowser.

I took that as my cue to leave and limped to the garage door. It wasn't open, but that was easily rectified.

As I reached it, I turned back to Bowser, "Bowser, break this door down." I rasped.

Bowser dropped the lifeless woman and took off, heading my way at full speed. He ran directly for the flimsy metal garage door and went straight through it, out into the Smog.

I hunched through the tattered hole he'd left and out into the grey once more; I hobbled after Bowser and soon found him, patiently waiting for me.

I looked around at the world and could only see grey. It was dark now, and the Smog was thick. I had no light, apart from that which spilt out of the garage behind me. I had no idea how I would get away. I was on the verge of collapse, and as I looked around, silver metal eyes began to stare back at me. Pair after pair shone out of the gloom, twenty, thirty pairs of eyes all trained on me. That's when the howling started.

A chill descended over my body, and my hands shook with a deep, primal fear. This was surely it for me. I took a knee; I had too. Just for a moment, to catch my breath, before the end. I lowered my head and closed my eyes, thinking, trying to figure a way out. I had nothing.

I opened my eyes, trying my best to ignore the howls, and saw something on the paved floor next to Bowser. It was a hoverboard—the same make and model as the boys. I chuckled and staggered toward it, and the howls grew louder. What are the odds this thing's broken, I thought? I knelt down, next to it, reached out a hand to the power switch on its base, and flicked it on.

The board ascended an inch off the ground and hovered happily. Without another thought, I jumped onto it and took off, screaming, "Bowser, make me a path through the vampires!"

Bowser bounded through two vampires, clearing me a way through. I pushed and pushed the hoverboard bringing it to its max speed as quickly as I could. I whizzed through the line of vampires and was away. Free from that house of horrors, at the centre of Hell City.

"Bowser, come!" I cried before my strength gave out, and I collapsed onto the board in a crouch, letting its momentum take me.

Bowser caught up to me; I grabbed his

metal tail and told him to run.

Chapter 11

The cold air blowing across my face kept me conscious, kept me holding on to Bowser. After a while, I managed to catch my breath and compose myself. We were running down the same road I'd come into the city on, as I'd hoped, and I knew we'd be finding the farm-house again soon. I wondered if anyone would come out, as it was the dead of night now visibility was down to nearly nothing and I was worried we'd walk right on by.

"Bowser, slow it down," I said, and he slowed to a trot.

I let go of the dog's tail, and feeling strong

enough, I managed to slowly board along next to him. It wasn't long before my worries vanished, and Rosie, the chicken flew out into the road and across my path once again. I feigned surprise and caught the chicken.

"Oh my god, where did you come from?" I said, and right on cue, a new old lady rushed out into the road.

I followed a similar script as the first time this happened, accepted the hospitality shown, and followed her around back and on into the house. This one's name was Gloria.

I told Bowser to wait outside for me and guard the house as Gloria shut the door behind us. I turned back and looked down at her with utter disdain, knowing what she had in stall for me—knowing what she'd likely already done to many others.

"Where's the phone?" I growled at her.

"Oh, honey, we don't have a phone here."

"Huh," I said. "Is that so? How'd you contact the vampires then?"

Gloria looked shocked, but I could see the edge of fear on her face.

"I-I don't know what you're talking about?" she stammered.

I'd had enough; I was tired, and hungry, and sick. "Tell me how you speak to them now, or I'll get the dog in here and get him to rip your traitorous throat out."

She held on for just a moment before breaking down and prattling on about how she was sorry, about how she didn't have a choice, blah, blah blah. After seeing what happened to people once the likes of Gloria and Jo are done, I had no sympathy whatsoever. I slapped her hard across the face.

"I don't care. Where's the phone?"

She told me it. It was an old satellite phone, one of the few remaining, I guessed.

"I'll make it easy for you," I said. "Leave now, without another word, take nothing and head away from the city. If you're lucky, you'll find some kind people who won't know about all the people you've sentenced to torture and likely death. Do that now, and I won't get the dog to rip you to pieces."

It was cruel, I know, but I needed her gone, and I needed to know she wouldn't be a threat. She opened her mouth to say something, but I raised my eyes at her, and she quickly closed it and scuttled out of the house crying.

"Bowser, follow her for a mile out of town; once she's gone, get back here as quick as you can," I said, and off he went as dutiful as ever.

With the house to myself, I could do no more. I stumbled up the stairs, and into the same bedroom I'd occupied before. I laid down and slept the sleep of the dead.

***

Morning came, and I awoke feeling a little better. Bowser sat next to my bed, and I knew I had at least a while to do what I needed to. I planned things out in my head; I knew Charles and his vampires would be after me and thought I'd maybe have the day before they realised Gloria was gone. I decided to work the day and make my move that night. I had one chance at this.

I needed energy, so I went out to the garden and found Rosie pecking away in her coup. It crossed my mind to break her neck and eat her, but the thought of the blood at once put me off. I grabbed the two eggs she'd laid and raided the cupboards. There wasn't much, but I found some more flatbreads, a little chard, and, of course, loads of mushrooms. I ate it all; in the back of my mind, I knew it would be my last meal, and I needed as much strength as I could get.

The next thing I knew, I was back in bed, upstairs. I had no idea how much time had passed and no idea how I'd got there. What I did know is that it seemed The Bronch had progressed a lot further than I wished it had. Especially for today, of all days. I was starting to lose myself. These blackouts would start becoming more frequent now, and I just prayed one wouldn't hit me again until the job was done. I got off the bed and went out to the shed.

"Follow me, Bowser; I have one job left for you."

I entered the cluttered shed again and marvelled at the car once more. I took a chance and popped the hood. Jo, the fucker, had lied to me. There was an engine in her, and it looked beautiful. It clearly hadn't been run much, judging by the shiny clean chrome. I opened the driver's side door and got in, checking the ignition for a key, no luck. I flipped down the sun visor—ha! Won't need that—but again, nothing. I checked the glove box last, but nothing in there either. As I was sitting back up, something caught my attention, under the passenger side footwell carpet. A bump in the carpet where one shouldn't have been, I fished around and pulled out a key.

I slid the key into the ignition, a massive grin on my face, and thought back to the kid again. To the day in the dump when we tried to find a working flux gear when I was looking for sunshine.

"I'm gonna give them all a bit of sunshine," I said to the empty room. "Here goes."

The engine coughed and groaned and then rumbled into life, I revved the engine once, and to my satisfaction, it roared, before quietening down to a happy purr.

"Yes!" I screamed, "Bowser, we're travelling in style!"

I got out of the car and finally got to work on my real task. I looked around the shed first, making sure everything I needed was here. It was like the vampires wanted to make a onestop vampire killing shop with this place; getting the residents of this place to store everything that could harm them in one place.

My first job was to make, what I liked to call, The Stake. Cheesy, you think, damn right, it's cheesy! The Stake was a high yield NNEMP bomb. Non-nuclear electromagnetic pulse, for those of you who are wondering. With a load of baked bean batteries and a bunch of other stuff, I was able to make an NNEMP that fit snuggly inside Bowser's body. At this size, it would only cover a couple of blocks of Hell City, but would, however, be powerful enough to permanently destroy the nano-robots inside of the vampires. That would go one of two ways. The nano-robots could simply short-circuit and die, effectively making the vampires entirely human again. Or they would create so much heat in such a short amount of time they would explosively short-circuit. The end result would be the same; the vampires would be vampires no longer and would have no need of all the people they had bound in The Precinct.

The NNEMP took me almost all of the day to make and fit within Bowser. The trigger was his jaw; one bite would trigger the EMP explosion. Without Bowser as my backup, without that brute force behind me, I needed something else. My luck held as there were the bodies of hundreds of robot guard dogs stored in the back of the shed. There were more than enough baked bean batteries and electromagnetic jaws to go round. My only problem was time. It had started getting dark by the time I'd finished the NNEMP, and I needed at least an hour's sleep before heading back to The Precinct. My cough had got worse, and I was now having coughing fits at least once an hour, which lasted a good five minutes. Because of this, I only rebuilt three dogs: Chase, Dylan, and Eve.

I got Bowser to wake me after an hour of sleep. By the time I was awake again, it was dark. The car was too small for all the dogs, but Chase, Dylan, and Eve would have no problem keeping up with Bowser and me in the car.

I revved the car into life, checked the fuel gauge was good, and hit the road. I drove with the headlights on. I was acting with abandon now; the car was pretty much a tank, and if any vampires got in my way, if the car didn't take them down, then the dogs behind would. I drove back into Hell City for the last time, vowing to leave it as Cell City once more.

Chapter 12

My foot was to the floor, and the engine was roaring like a lion as we entered the city. Bowser sat next to me, mouth agape, waiting, in the passenger seat. Buildings started whizzing past us, each reaching further up into the sky, higher and higher, fingers of humanity clawing through the Smog, reaching for sunshine. The few people or vampires on the street whipped past us like groaning ghosts.

I couldn't see the building, but I felt The Precinct nearing, a building that was topped with a huge, hollow copper globe. One that, once upon a time, glowed like the sun, a beckon of hope for the city. I hoped to reignite that hope tonight. Then, suddenly there it was. The metal garage door was down, but I pushed on through tripling the size of the hole Bowser had made the previous day. I watched the rear-view mirror as Chase, Dylan, and Eve all jumped through the hole and into the garage behind me.

I drove around the garage, revving the engine as much as I could, then I slammed on the breaks. If the revving didn't do it, then the scream of the tires announced my arrival. The smoke they kicked out gave the garage the same spooky feel of the Smog outside.

I shifted the car into park, swung the door open, and stepped out. The smell of burning rubber filled my nose and I loved it, despite the tickle it raised in the back of my throat. I pushed it down, took a deep breath, and waited for all hell to break loose.

I looked down to the opposite end of the garage, and again, there were two hover-trucks waiting. I told the dogs—who'd I'd programmed to take commands individually, or as a group, I'd christened C-DE—to go and disable the hover-trucks. If there was blood in them, I didn't want it going any further. Bowser sat at my side, patiently waiting for his commands.

It didn't take long for a few vampires to come out of hiding to see what all the noise was. A small group entered the garage and clocked me. One of the group said something to the rest that I couldn't make out, then retreated back into the building.

The rest slowly made their way over toward me.

"You're the girl causing all the trouble, aren't you?" One of them said.

"Charles isn't very happy about what you did to Giles," another chimed in.

"I'd stay where you are if I was you," I shouted, trying to sound authoritative and confident. They were still fifty or so yards away. "Unless you wanna end up just like Charles?"

"You and one measly dog cannot take all five of us down at once," the first vampire said and then made a move for me. It triggered the others to run too.

"C-DE, to me," I shouted.

The trio of dogs was back by my side before the vampires made half the distance. I laughed and said, "You still think you can take me?"

They looked from one to the other, unsure of themselves, until all eyes fell on the leader of the pack. He lifted his head, full of arrogance and self-importance. "You're just a dying, little girl and her dogs, get her!"

"C-DE, protect me," I shouted. The trio padded a few steps in front of me, ready.

The first vampire reached the dogs and as soon as they tried to get past Eve clamped down on their leg. Just on the first's tail, the next two were caught by Chase and Dylan. Within seconds all the nano-robots were drawn from their bodies, leaving them bloodied and ruined on the floor.

The leader of the group and the last lackey stopped in their tracks, terrified at the power of my dogs.

"Just a poor little girl and her pups, huh?" I goaded.

The leader snarled at me but started to back up. "You won't get away with this."

Fuck these guys. Fuck em all. Maybe I should have been merciful, but for all the pain they'd caused, they didn't deserve it. If that cursed me, if that was gonna send me to hell soon, then so be it; it'd be worth it just to save one of the poor souls imprisoned here.

"Chase, Dylan. Kill em both." I whispered, stifling a cough.

"Noooo!" screamed the leader, his voice high pitched and wretched.

Finally, alone, I coughed my guts up, once more. Spitting out a grey mess of phlegm, I composed myself, took a deep breath, and left the garage and five bloody piles of flesh behind me.

***

I was right in my thoughts that the place would not be well guarded. The vampires were not used to having people stand against them and never thought to protect themselves. That was good for me, and one of the reasons I was relatively happy with just the three additional dogs to back me up. I told Chase and Dylan to lead the way up the steps, we had a long way to go, and the only way was up. I clambered onto Bowsers back, my arms gripped tightly around his neck, and Eve brought up the rear, protecting us from both directions.

It was well known, when the world had only been slowly dying, rather than in its death throes that the top floor of The Precinct was a massive office space reserved for the chief of police. It was meant to be a magnificent room, and I choose this as the place to execute my plan for two reasons.

First, I hoped being so close to the top of the tower and the bronze globe that stood atop it, that when I triggered the EMP bomb, the bronze globe would act to enhance the bombs reach.

Secondly, I expected this to be where Charles would now be residing, and I had unfinished business with that arsehole.

Time seemed to lose all meaning as we ascended. Round and round we went, floor after floor passed. The 13th floor passed; the bloody mess remained on the landing. The 111th floor passed, where I had spent so much time trying not to lose my mind. But now it was starting to go, the next time I looked up I saw we were at the 220th floor. I'd just lost over a hundred floors in an instant to The Bronch, I felt lucky I'd not fallen off Bowser, but at the same time, I was terrified the next time I might blackout was at the crucial moment. Up and up, we continued, seeing not a soul, no nurses, no cleaners, no muscle.

Finally, we all reached the summit—the 250th floor. I would have died getting up there if I had had to walk it, that's a fact, but I had Bowser, and when we reached the landing of the floor, I was finally able to get off of Bowser's back. He wasn't fazed, but my back was killing me, and my arms ached thanks to all the jostling. I stretched my back out and looked around the landing, it was bare, the same as all the rest. My throat was dry and tickly, I couldn't help but cough, no doubt giving away my presence if anyone was up here. I took a drink; it helped my throat but did nothing to alleviate the butterflies that fluttered about my stomach. I was under no illusion that this may well be the last few moments for me, but I wasn't long for this earth anyway, so I wanted to do some good before I left it.

I wanted a really kick-ass movie entrance, and so I silently opened the door by the handles, just a crack, before booting them opening and entering the huge office. I must have looked sweaty and tired and beat up, and like a real bad ass too as I strutted in.

What met me took my breath away. It wasn't the large windows that lined the walls and the thought of the views this room would have should the Smog clear, that stole my breath. Nor was it the beautiful landscape paintings from a time before the Smog that hung between each window on a small piece of wall space. It wasn't the antique mahogany table that Charles sat behind, it wasn't even the thirty or so vampires that occupied the room.

What took my breath away was the sight of Henry lying unconscious across a coffee table in front of Charles' desk, between two leather sofas. His face was battered and bruised, his eyes swollen shut. The fingers on his hands stood crooked, pointing the opposite direction to which they should. He had no shirt on, and his chest was crisscrossed with the lacerations of a whipping. Not only that but he looked completely emaciated, as if he hadn't eaten in weeks. His ribs were prominent enough to count, his face gaunt and hollow. My stomach lurched, and it took everything within me to not be sick.

"Cyra! So good of you to join the party,"

Charles said. "Please, don't say a word. You do, and I cut dear Henry's head clean off." A guard stood by some sort of sword in hand, eager to fulfil his boss's request.

A guttural cough started, not me this time, and not one born of The Bronch. This was Henry coughing up blood as he came to. The room all turned to look at him as he pulled himself unsteadily up and into a sitting position on the coffee table. He spat a big red globule of blood onto the wood floor and looked up, squinting between eyes forced shut thanks to swelling.

"Hey Cyra," he said and coughed some more. "I'm glad you got out. Glad you managed to take a few of these sick fucks too."

"Oh Jesus, Henry," I said, "what have they done to you?"

"Oh, this? This is nothing; I haven't eaten since we talked. Fuck these fucks and fuck those robots in my blood."

"Will you please shut up?" Charles cut in, becoming impatient.

"Fuck you, Charles," Henry said and leapt up, diving over the table, arms outstretched, looking for Charles' neck.

Henry groped at his neck aimlessly, his

battered and broken fingers unable to get any purchase.

"Kill the boy," Charles laughed. "Just kill him."

The lackey with the sword strolled up behind the outstretched Henry and drove the sword down in Henry's back. I heard a sickening crack as it broke through his ribs, and then a dull thud as the sword impaled itself in the desk.

"Careful of the desk, for god's sake," Charles spat.

I gasped in shock, seeing Henry brutally murdered in cold blood.

Charles pushed his chair away from the desk and stood. The lackey withdrew the sword, and Charles flipped Henry over. Henry didn't have an expression of fear or anger on his face; he had one of happiness, knowing he'd been released from his hell on earth. My heart warmed, and my resolve hardened at this. In the short commotion, I looked at the brood of vampires in the room and realised then why my journey up had been so easy, it was because Charles had gathered his forces in his stronghold, here. Part of me delighted in that fact, knowing what I was about to do. My mouth opened about to command the dogs when Charles screamed at me.

"Don't even think about it," he barked. He then turned back and called out, "Bring him forward."

My blood ran cold as Vic was pushed through the group of vampires to the fore. He too was beaten, both his eyes black and his lip split, but thankfully he was in nowhere near as bad a shape as Henry. "We found this fellow creeping around our home here. It didn't take long for Henry to give the man up," Charles said and chuckled. "Mr. Vic, somewhat of a surrogate father figure."

"Vic," I whispered to myself, how... why... what are you doing here? I wondered.

"Now, unless you want me to kill another of your Daddies, the next thing you're going to do is tell the dogs to sit down and de-activate."

The look of Charles' face was one of smugness, a pure and unfiltered joy in the knowing that he'd beaten me.

"C-DE, Bowser," I started. "Sit down and deactivate." I slumped to my knees, buried my face in my hands, and cried.

Footsteps echoed off the polished wood floor as they came closer and closer. I knew it would be Charles, now confident in the fact he was safe from the dogs.

"Cyra, Cyra, Cyra. Whatever am I to do with you?" he said and stroked my hair.

"Get the fuck off me, Charles, you sick fuck," I screamed, sitting up and batting his hand away.

He took a step back, a little shocked. He quickly regained his composure and stood next to Bowser, kneeling down, looking into his open maw. He feigned fear before placing a hand on Bowser's head, leaning on the dog like he was nothing more than a table. "Charles!" he barked, the joviality back in his voice. "Please, I go by The Count now."

I burst out laughing. I just couldn't help myself. "The Count! That's amazing; you're not even a vampire. You're as human as I am, you just have a few million robots swimming about your blood. You, Charlie, you're nothing more than a glorified fucking cannibal. You sick fuck."

Stars flashed in my vision as Charles brought down a vicious backhand across my face. "Careful Cyra, one more outburst like that, and dear old Daddy two will get it." Charles growled.

I rubbed my cheek and drew in a breath through gritted teeth. "The hell are you doing here?" I shouted at Vic, so angry I wanted to scream.

"I'm sorry, Cyra," Vic slurred through his fat, split lip. "I've been following since you left. I saw Henry be kind to you; I gave him your bag; I even left the hoverboard for you. I wanted to help you. Keep you safe. You're all I have left now. I love you."

I looked to Vic, my eyes tearing up. I looked to the bloodied mess, which was Henry. I knew what I had to do.

"I love you too, Vic. You know what? I think Thomas-"

That's when all hell really did break loose. You see, I had pre-empted some potential hiccups in my plan and added a contingency. I programmed all the dogs with a one-word back up command. A word I tried never to use, one that brought up too many emotions and memories—the boy's name. I set C-DE to kill any vampires they detected, and I set Bowser to clamp his jaw down on the nearest vampire, which just so happened to be Charles.

C-DE leapt into action and killed absolutely no one.

Bowser moved first Charles' hand was resting in the dog's head, Bowser turned in an instant and clamped down on Charles' forearm.

The NNEMP detonated. A wave of energy flew through the room. A tingling sensation flooded me for just a second and was gone. The room turned pitch black as the electrics went.

I heard the metallic bang as Bowser, Chase, Dylan, and Eve all slumped to the floor, lifeless; the EMP short-circuiting them.

I heard Charles scream, as did all the other vampires in the room.

Hate filled me at that moment; a burning hot rage flowed in my very veins as I looked in Charles' metallic eyes piercing the darkness. Fear and pain were all I could see in them, and then they turned from silver to red. I started to see the veins in his neck pulse as they began to glow a warm orange. Still, his scream increased, and the orange veins started to darken. I realised what was happening. The nano-robots, thanks to the EMP, were overheating and exploding in his bloodstream. A million or more tiny explosions were ripping him to shreds from the inside out.

His whole body glowed and began to expand outwards. For a second, I thought he might explode, but thankfully that never happened. The veins glowed orange and then black before the heat became too much, and he burst into flames. They all did. Thirty-odd vampires were screaming in agony, bursting into flame like a vampire stepping into daylight, stepping into the sunshine.

I had a brief moment of utter jubilation flow over me before I fell into an unknown darkness once more.

Chapter 13

From then on, my life became like a living montage; in the most part, I was only able to grab fleeting instants of clarity. I did, however, get a few more extended moments of being myself.

I next came to with Vic carrying me down the stairs of The Precinct. He'd found my backpack, it was full of chemical light sticks, and he held one in his mouth, lighting our way. We were only a few floors down. It was, in fact, the highest floor that housed the herd. He put me down, and we both entered the stinking room that now also had another smell to it—

the smell of cooked pork. As we walked in, a vampiric nurse was ablaze in one of the aisles. Vic grabbed a fire extinguisher as I set about freeing people, telling them to pay it forward. The people, they were weak, so weak. But their freedom gave them a newfound energy, and they all cheered for their liberation. They cheered for the death of their captors too.

Later.

I was stood next to Vic in the street outside The Precinct. A flood of humanity was pouring out the doors in all directions. They rubbed at chaffed wrists and limped around, weak and tired, unsure where exactly to go, but, above all, they were happy. I told Vic about the car I came in; we went to it and drove away from that wretched building forever. Guilt gripped me as we left, knowing these people had nothing and no one to help them. I'd given them their freedom, though, and now the rest was down to them.

Later.

I was sat at a desk, a light-stick laying in front of me. I raised the stick and looked around. I was in the Cell City Central Library. The building was massive; huge white marble columns and arches lined the walls, each leading to stacks of books.

"Vic!" I shouted.

Footsteps echoed throughout the room, and I saw a light walking back toward me.

"Vic?"

"I got it," Vic shouted, waving a book above his head.

"Got what?"

"Did you forget why you came to the city in the first place?"

My mind was clouding over once again; thoughts and reason got harder to hold on to. I fought the fog in my head and remembered.

"The Smog?" I whispered to myself, remembering, "The Sky Whale."

"Exactly!" Vic said as he returned, "and now I know where we need to go."

Later.

Smog whipped by the window of the car as Vic drove.

"Where are we going?" I croaked. Breathing was a constant battle now.

"Welcome back," Vic said, looking at me with a smile on his face. "The mountains."

"How far do we need to go?

"Far enough."

Later.

The Smog was not as thick the next time I came to, and I could see wide open plains. It was the furthest I'd seen maybe ever. I was sat on yellow grass; a campfire lit in front of me. Before I could say a word, a wretched, wet cough ripped through me. Vic rushed to my side, patted my back, and offered me some water. My arms and legs felt so heavy, every movement was a battle, but I lifted the water and swallowed. It helped, and I was able to talk.

"What happens to me?" It was all I could manage, but thankfully Vic understood.

"Depends," he started. He briefly glanced at me and offered me a pitying smile. The pain it caused him watching me like this was clear to see. "The good times, you just sleep. The bad, you scream, calling for your parents, me, Henry a couple times. And..." he trailed off. It was still too painful for him. "Or you wander aimlessly," he continued. "I've nearly lost you a couple of times. Please just stay put, okay?" he said and gave me a playful push.

I smiled; trying not to laugh.

"Sorry," I croaked, "Backpack?"

Vic looked around and passed me my backpack.

I followed his gaze around camp and noticed that the car was gone. "Car?"

"Ran outta gas."

I nodded, expecting that sooner or later. I dug around the bag and pulled out a journal. It was one I'd written back while fixing up Bowser and C-DE, it had notes on how to build the NNEMPs. I handed it to Vic.

Vic looked at me quizzically and thumbed through the journal. Realisation dawned on his face. I knew when I was gone; he'd have nothing to live for. So, I gave him something. He shook his head, but I saw in his eyes that he would do it. He'd fight back and take as many vampires down before the end.

"What were you gonna say?" Vic asked me.

I shrugged my shoulders, puzzled.

"Back in The Precinct? Before the bomb went off."

I smiled at him and nodded. Slowly I unscrewed the lid off the water and lubricated my throat once more. As I put the bottle back in my backpack, I felt the gloves; I pulled them out, waved them at Vic, and put them on. "Thomas... he'd be proud of us."

Vic's face cracked, and I saw him cry for the first time. It set me off too. We were both crying for everything we'd lost.

"I'm sorry," he said after a while. "I sat idly by and watched you both die. Thomas had too much energy, always forgetting his mask, and you were too consumed with your work. I should have made sure you were both wearing those god-damned masks. I killed you both." With that, he dropped his face into his huge hands and cried again.

I got myself up, on unsteady feet and slowly made my way over to him. Sitting next him, I put my arms round him and hugged. When he finally looked back up, I took his hands in mine, squeezed them and shook my head. He smiled down at me and hugged me back.

"Yeah," Vic said after a while, in a cracked and broken voice. "He would. And I'm proud of you too, kid."

It was the last thing I heard before drifting off into blackness again.

The last time I came to, I felt an odd

warmth all over my body. I was lying on a bed of green grass, Vic was nowhere to be seen, and mountains towered above me. Mountains, I could see them, and beyond their peaks, a glorious blue sky. I cried again. Happy tears. Then, from around one of the peaks, I watched as a huge sky whale emerged, its mouth agape, thin tail waving out behind. I held my hands to my face and felt the gloves caress my cheeks and once more thought of Thomas, the boy, the kid. I watched as another sky whale floated into view, followed by another and then another, all the while I was being bathed in warm, comforting sunshine.

Author's Note

Beta readers are the best. If you've ever written and you've never used beta readers, I urge you, get on the internets, the socials, your library, whatever, just find someone like minded who you'd be happy to swap stories with and hone your craft with them.

This story would not even be here if not for my beta readers. It started off very different. Sunshine was only a one-hundred word drabble. A beta reader friend pointed me toward a free online drabble class. Its goal, get you writing a complete story with a clear beginning, middle and end in just one hundred words. The original Sunshine was one of five stories to come out of that course.

Another beta reader loved Sunshine in particular, helped me hone it and suggested there may be more to it. That a whole world had been created in just one-hundred words and that maybe Cyra's story wasn't over.

It stuck with me and grew and grew in my head, until I realised that drabble was just a prologue of sorts, the start of Cyra's journey. And so, I picked up the pen and continued to write. 22k words later, more invaluable help from yet another beta reader and you're holding the results in your hands.

I sincerely hope that you've enjoyed Cyra's journey across some pretty bleak lands. If you have, please consider injecting a little light into my day and leave the story a review up on Amazon and/or Goodreads.

This is my first solo novella and I have to thank all the people who helped make my dream a reality. You know who you are. But a special shout out to my wife, Carley, for putting up with the keyboard clicks night and night.

Until next time (hopefully they'll be a next time!),

L. T. Emery

About the Author

L. T. Emery is a British author, with a love for Horror, Sci-fi and Fantasy genres.

He is the proud father of one and husband to the love of his life. Outside of family life, he is an avid reader of novels, genre magazines, comics, manga and just about anything else he can get his hands on. With a particular love of long form fiction, he is currently working on a fantasy novel which he hopes to publish in the future. He can be found online at
https://ltemery.wixsite.com/home
and twitter.com/ltemeryuk

More From Nordic Press

Novels/Novellas

Face of Fear by C. Marry Hultman
9789198671001

Dawson Junior G3 by Brian Wagstaff
9789198671049

Boy in the Wardrobe by Esther Jacoby
9789198684018

New Life Cottage by Esther Jacoby
9789198671056

The Wait by Esther Jacoby
e-book:https://books2read.com/u/4Dgz8Q

Liebe ist Warten by Esther Jacoby
9789198671070

Das Cottage by Ester Jacoby
9789198684070

Musing on Death & Dying by Esther Jacoby
9789198671063

Earth Door by Cye Thomas
9789198671025

An Odd Collection of Tales By Cye Thomes
9789198684124

Graffiti Stories by Nick Gerrard
9789198671018

Punk Novelette by Nick Gerrard
9789198671087

Struggle and Strife by Nick Gerrard
9789198684049

Fake Escape by Natalie Hughes
e-book:https://books2read.com/u/bMXL5X

Cold as Hell by Neen Cohen
9789198684094

Hell Hath No Fury by Chisto Healy
9789198750706

True Mates by E.F. Vogel
9789198750713

9 789198 750942